BATMAN IN
Terror on the
High Skies

by Joe R. Lansdale

*Illustrated by Edward Hannigan
and Dick Giordano*

Little, Brown and Company
Boston Toronto London

For Kasey and Keith Lansdale

First Edition

ISBN 0-316-17765-2
Library of Congress Catalog Card Number 92-56756
Library of Congress Cataloging-in-Publication information is available.

10 9 8 7 6 5 4 3 2 1

AR-BUF

Printed in the United States of America

CHAPTER ONE

The Flying Ship

You'd have to say I got into this whole scary business by accident, meeting Batman and all, and being involved in one of his more important cases. Important to me anyway, on account of it's the only real mystery I've had anything to do with. Though when I get older, you can be certain I'll be involved with others. Take up crime fighting like Batman, but without the cape and all. There can only be one Batman, no matter how hard I might want to be like him.

Then again, there's only one me, Toby Tyler, which is the same name as the book character who ran away to join the circus, or something like that. I wouldn't know for sure. I've never read, or seen, the book about Toby Tyler. But Mom says that's where the name comes from, Dad having the last name Tyler and her thinking the Toby name would fit me. Or to put it her way, she thought, "It would be cute."

Spare me cute. A bunny is cute. Me, I'm Toby Tyler, and

I don't think you want to call a full-sized eleven-year-old who once helped Batman out on some important matters, cute.

But I was talking about how I came to meet Batman.

We had moved to Gotham about six months before from a farm just outside a little East Texas town called Mud Creek, and I wished we hadn't. I didn't like the city at all.

It wasn't what I expected, and I hadn't expected much. This time I'm talking about, the city was hot. Somehow, moving up North, I thought even in the summer it would be cold. But it wasn't. It was hot. Hot as East Texas.

And there were all these people, pushing, shoving, and fussing at one another. Say "howdy" or "excuse me," they look at you like you've just dropped in from Mars.

I hadn't been able to make a single friend. The kids I met called me hick, played games I'd never seen, and didn't know anything about fishing. To them the woods was a place where lumber grew.

I often wished I was back in East Texas on our old farm with my fishing line thrown off in our creek. But Dad had been in a bad way down in Texas, what with four years of drought back to back and no jobs to be had anywhere about. So we came here on account of an old friend of Dad's, Mr. Jim Gordon, had written and given him a tip about a job that paid pretty well, even if a lot of it went out to pay for rent and food.

Jim Gordon was the Police Commissioner of Gotham City. My dad had known him when they were younger and Dad had lived here and gone to the Police Academy, thinking he wanted to be a policeman. But Dad decided he didn't

2

want to be a policeman after all, and had gone back to East Texas, back to farming, like his dad. But now, here we were, and Dad was a night watchman for a warehouse over by the boat docks. He didn't like it as well as farming, but for the time being, it certainly paid better.

Mr. Gordon came over and visited with us a lot. I liked him. He and Mom and Dad would play cards, and he and Dad would talk about when they were in the academy together. Sometimes Mr. Gordon would talk about Batman, who was a good friend of his. It was kind of neat that Mr. Gordon was Batman's friend and my dad's friend, too.

One hot night Mr. Gordon came over to our place to have dinner. Our place is this apartment about four stories up in a five-story building that has all the personality of a cardboard box full of wet dirt.

About eight, Mom sent me off to brush my teeth and go to my room while the adults played cards and talked. I really wanted to stay up and hear any stories they might tell, but Mom wasn't having any of that. I went to my room and hung out, tried to hear what they were talking about in the kitchen, which I couldn't do too well on account of the door to my bedroom was pretty thick and they had a fan going in there. I had one going in my window, too, and I wasn't about to cut it off. It was too hot for that.

I finally gave up trying to hear what they were talking about, got out some of my books and looked them over. I had read all of them, some twice, and I still remembered them a little too well to reread. I put the books up and got out my box of comics and tried looking over those, but they weren't doing much for me either. I just wasn't in the mood.

I found an article Mom had cut out of the *Gotham Times* for me about a movie they were making in the city. A sea monster movie called *The Behemoth,* starring an actor named Shelly D. Bloon. I had a lot of magazines with articles on Shelly D. Bloon. He was my favorite horror movie actor.

The article told that a giant mechanical sea monster had been built for *The Behemoth*. It was the first of its kind, controlled by a man inside its head who drove it with a stick shift and buttons. It could perform in a way no movie monster had performed before. The article called it a modern miracle.

I put the article down. It was interesting, but it was too hot to concentrate, and I even realized, though I had read all of it, I could only remember the first half. I was reading it without really seeing it. I kept thinking about the heat and my friends back in Texas, wondering what they were doing this summer.

I wondered if they were catching lots of fish. I wondered if the grass had grown up tall on our farm. I wondered if the squirrels Mom used to feed out by the bird feeder were still coming around looking for sunflower seeds. I wondered how long it would be before we got enough money saved up to go back home and try farming again. I wondered if we ever would.

I got tired of thinking about all that. I went over to the window where the fan was and stood right in front of it and let the wind blow my hair up and swirl down my collar.

While I was standing there, looking through the slats of the fan, I saw a shadow and the shadow moved and flicked and then there was a scream from the building across the way.

The scream was like a cat makes when it's in pain or frightened. In fact, I was pretty certain that's what it was, a cat.

I figured my parents and Mr. Gordon hadn't heard the scream, what with them in the other room and the fans running and all, so I turned off my fan and set it on the floor and stepped through the open window onto the old-fashioned fire escape.

I knew I wasn't supposed to be out there, but while I stood there considering how much trouble I was going to get into if I got caught, the scream came again, and this time I could tell it was a cat, and that it was somewhere on the roof across the way, about a story higher than where I was. I couldn't let an animal suffer. I had to do something.

I turned and looked up at our building, saw that if I put a foot on the railing that ran around the fire escape, I could get hold of a gargoyle that stuck out above me, get on top of it, step up to a higher window ledge, and from there, get hold of another gargoyle and boost myself onto the roof.

Without really thinking about it, I climbed onto the railing, jumped, grabbed the first gargoyle, pulled myself onto it, and stood up. I stretched and grabbed hold of the window ledge above it and pulled myself up. Dust and pigeon droppings flew off the ledge and went sailing out into the night. Suddenly I wished I was back in my room reading comic books or finishing up that article on *The Behemoth*.

But I couldn't get the cat out of my mind, and that he might be in pain. I felt I'd gone this far, I might as well make the whole trip. I got myself onto the window ledge and grabbed the sides of the window frame and didn't look down. I tried not to think how I was going to get back to the fire escape.

The cat screamed again.

I angled my body as much as possible, and jumped up hard, grabbed hold of the second gargoyle and tugged myself on top of it without my arms coming off at the shoulders. I stood up slowly and took hold of the edge of the roof and scrambled on top of the building and rolled over on my back and sucked in a deep breath and let it out easy.

I lay there for a moment, breathing in the hot night air, watching the smog move around in the sky, temporarily blocking the gold, full moon. When I got my wind and gumption back, I stood up and looked across the way. Another scream leaped through the night and filled my ears.

I could see this big tin vent pipe on the building over there, sticking up from the center of the roof. I could see something flicking about in the mouth of the vent, like a long, fuzzy tongue.

A moment later, the smog cleared and the moon shone brighter, and I could see it was a cat's tail. The silly critter had crawled in there and gotten stuck, and now he was yelling down the vent for help and thrashing his tail like it was some kind of flag.

There was a six-foot-wide gap between the roof of my building and the roof where the cat was stuck, and I eyed those six feet suspiciously. Back home I used to do a lot of running and jumping, and I was known for the longest leap among the kids. But those leaps were running leaps from the ground, where the worst thing that could happen was I'd land in the sand.

Here, if I miscalculated, missed my footing, there was a long drop between me and the narrow alley below.

I thought it over and decided if I didn't look down and just ran for all I was worth and gave it my best jump, it would be a piece of cake.

I backed up and took off, ran hard and leaped. I landed on the roof of the other building, hit my foot in some water puddled there, slipped and skidded, and scraped my knee.

I got up and shook out my leg, trying to throw off the pain. I limped over and looked in the vent at the cat. All I could see of him was his tail thrashing. I reached in and got hold of him, but he wouldn't budge. He was hanging on with his claws and swelling his sides so much he was stuck in there tight as a ripe cucumber in a water hose.

While I was trying to get the cat loose, I saw the moon's reflection in a puddle of water on the roof, and then I saw something else in the puddle but couldn't believe what it was.

I turned and looked at the sky, and there, sailing across the face of the great, gold moon, was a huge pirate ship, complete with fluttering, black sails.

CHAPTER TWO

Walking the Plank

The ship was carried aloft by a zeppelin, and painted on the front of the zeppelin was a grinning skull-white face with green hair, red lips, and teeth white as snow.

The ship dipped forward and started down toward the roof where I stood. The moonlight was clear and gold and it outlined the ship and made its edges shimmer with a ghostly glow. I thought I was dreaming, but right then the cat showed me I wasn't. The ungrateful rascal backed out of the vent and screeched and scratched me and ran off.

I put my hand to my mouth and sucked at the scratch. It hurt. That proved to me I wasn't dreaming. I was wide awake. That pirate ship was about to dock right in front of me. It settled on the roof. An anchor and chain shot out of the side of the ship, hit the roof hard, and stuck there. A white face appeared at the railing. Part of the railing swung open like a gate, and a ramp was lowered.

Then the strangest man I've ever seen came down the ramp. His was the face painted on the front of the zeppelin.

9

He was tall and lean, and wore a purple pirate's outfit with bright green leather knee-high boots, and purple trousers with green trim. He had on a purple pirate's hat pushed back on his head so that I could see some of his hair, and it was the color of green persimmons. His blood-red lips were drawn back in his pale face in a wide, crazy smile. He was carrying a cutlass, or what looked like one at first glance, but was in fact some kind of light chainsaw made to look like a cutlass. A huge green parrot was perched on his right shoulder.

I knew who he was immediately, of course. I had known the moment I had seen his face on the zeppelin. How could I not know? His picture had been all over the newspapers and television, since his recent escape from Arkham Asylum. It was the mad criminal clown they called *the Joker*.

Walking down the ramp behind him were a woman and two men. They, too, were dressed like pirates, and they acted as if they'd rather not be dressed that way. They looked embarrassed and uncomfortable.

The woman pirate was very muscular, like a bodybuilder. She wore a patch over one eye. She had a rope coiled over her shoulder, and dangling from that was a grappling hook. The hook winked in the moonlight.

One of the male pirates was short and so fat he was almost round. He walked like there was something sharp in his shoes. The other pirate was bony as a skeleton. He walked as if his legs and arms were being worked by puppet strings. Both men carried empty canvas bags.

On board ship, several more pirates stood staring over the railing.

10

The Joker stepped off the ramp and onto the roof. He looked at me and cocked a green eyebrow.

"Well, me matie," he said. "Seems you've lost yer bearin's. Arrr, arrr."

The Joker tilted his head like a curious puppy. He seemed to be waiting for something that didn't come. If he was waiting on me to speak, he was out of luck. I was too startled. But that wasn't it. He turned to his gang.

"Arrr, arrr," he said.

His gang had finished coming off the ramp and were standing behind him, shuffling their feet. "Arrr, arrr," they all said together, but not like they really meant it.

The Joker sighed. He looked at me and shook his head. He looked at the moon and shook his head. He looked back at his gang.

"All right," he said, "listen up. This is the last time I tell you. It's no fun if you don't do it right. We're pirates, see. We look like pirates. We act like pirates. And we talk like pirates. Right, Polly?"

Polly didn't do anything. The Joker reached up and got hold of something on Polly's belly and pulled. It was a string. I realized then Polly wasn't real. Polly was a toy. When the Joker let go of the string, the parrot said, "Attsss right. The Joker's always right."

Polly's voice was the Joker's voice. There must have been a tape player inside the toy parrot.

The Joker turned to his gang. "Am I getting through here?"

"Gee," said the round pirate, "I don't know, boss. I feel kind of silly, you know. Arrr, arrin' and all that. And this outfit and stuff, it's really hot. Besides, don't you think we ought to worry about the kid there?"

"Oh, the kid," said the Joker. "*You're* worried about the kid. You're saying *I'm* not concerned?"

The round pirate became nervous. "No, boss. I ain't saying that."

"Say you aren't?" said the Joker, and he was smiling big. But the smile wasn't comforting. It was like looking a shark in the mouth.

The Joker reached out with one hand and adjusted the round pirate's shirt collar. "You wouldn't be turning into a landlubber, would you, me bucko?"

The pirate had begun to sweat. "No, sir. Arrr, arrr, sir."

"Good," said the Joker. "That's better. But those arr, arrs could use some work. Make them real sea dog–type arrr, arrrs. From the heart. Hear what I'm trying to tell you?"

"Aye, aye, sir," the pirate said, saluting. "Arrr, arrr!"

"Very nice," said the Joker. "Well done. I'm pleased."

I was thinking of running and jumping back to my building, but I was so startled by the pirate ship landing on the roof, I was glued to my spot.

The Joker strolled over to me, smiling. He reached out with the chainsaw cutlass and touched my chest with it.

"Hey, little matie," he said. "Don't be scared. I'm Captain Joker, and you and me, we're gonna play pirate. You'd like that, wouldn't you?"

I didn't think so, but I didn't say anything.

"Seems odd ye be up here this time of night, standing

about on this roof . . . this island . . . with your mouth hanging open. Arrr, arrr."

His gang chimed in behind him. "Arrr, arrr!"

I said something about the cat. I don't remember what I said exactly. I was scared.

"A cat?" said the Joker. "That's sweet. Really." He leaned close to me. "And now we'll be about taking our booty."

"Shaking our booty?" said the woman pirate.

The Joker turned and glared at the woman. "Booty is pirate talk for treasure, knucklehead. If I said we're going to shake our booty, that would be dancing. We've come to steal booty, not shake our booty. Okay?"

"Arrr, arrr," said the gang.

The Joker leaned close to me and whispered, "The crooks these days. It's like they haven't got a brain among them."

Suddenly the Joker jerked the sword high above his head, as if to strike. But at the last moment he giggled and reached up with his other hand and pulled a cord in the handle of the cutlass and fired the chainsaw to life. He whirled, crouched, and swung the sword low and level. He hit the tin vent close to where it joined the building and sawed through it in a matter of seconds, sparks jumping from the saw and metal like fiery Mexican jumping beans. The Joker cut the engine on the saw and yelled, "Bony!"

Bony, as you might have guessed, was the thin, male pirate. The woman pirate tossed Bony the rope and hook. He fastened the hook and dropped the rope down the narrow shaft. He tossed his empty canvas bag over his shoulder and squeezed into the opening in the roof, took hold of the rope, and slipped down and out of sight, easy as a greased snake.

The Joker turned and smiled at me. "Bloody Mary," he said.

The muscular woman pirate pulled a strip of leather out of her outfit and stuck it between her teeth, then she moved. She moved fast. One minute she was beside the Joker, the next she was behind me. She grabbed my arms and jerked them behind my back. I struggled, but she was too strong. She tied my wrists together with the strip of leather, then held me by the arm so I couldn't run away.

"Hey, boss," said the round pirate. "Bony's tugging on the rope."

"Well, pull it up, you nitwit," said the Joker.

"Yeah, right," said the round pirate. He bent with difficulty and got hold of the rope and pulled it out of the shaft. It stuck when it came to the end, and the round pirate struggled a bit to free the canvas bag.

The bag was no longer empty. It was stuffed fat as the shaft would allow. The round pirate set the full bag aside, and tied his empty bag to the rope and lowered it.

The Joker said to the round pirate, "Cannon Ball, get me the plank."

"Arrr, arrr," said Cannon Ball. The little round man seemed to roll across the rooftop, up the plank of the ship, and back again. Only when he returned, he was carrying a long, narrow board with him. He walked to the edge of

14

the building and placed the board on the roof so that most of the board stuck out into the darkness. He held it there with one fat foot.

The Joker came over and put his foot on the board. Cannon Ball went back to the shaft and said, "Bony's tugging the rope again."

"Pull it up again, you fool," the Joker said.

"Oh, yeah," said Cannon Ball, and he tugged the rope up. The second bag was tied to the end of it, and it, too, was full. Cannon Ball removed the bag and dropped the rope back down the shaft. Bony scuttled up the rope and out of the hole fast as a spider. He removed the hook from the roof and coiled the rope over his shoulder.

"All done?" asked the Joker.

"All done, sir," said Bony.

"Good," said the Joker. "Oh, little boy, would you come over here, please?"

No one actually waited for me to come over. Bloody Mary jerked me over to the roof's edge and pushed me out on the board. The Joker moved his foot slightly so that the board shook. "Scary, huh?" said the Joker. He put the tip of his chainsaw cutlass in the small of my back and prodded me with it. I walked out on the plank.

It was terrifying to be out there on that thin board, over the deep darkness. I tried not to look down.

"Walk the plank, me bucko," said the Joker.

But I didn't move. I couldn't move. I was terrified.

"Well, then," said the Joker, "yo-ho-ho and a kid made of mush. Bon voyage, matie."

The Joker took his foot off his end of the board, and I fell into darkness.

As I went over the side, I heard Cannon Ball say something to the Joker that sounded like, "And now for the bean heat mouth in shiny the balloon," but I was uncertain. My mind was a tad occupied. I was hurtling to my doom, down the long, dark drop to the alley floor below.

CHAPTER THREE

Three Cards of Crime

A great black bird flapped out of the night and hit me.

No. Grabbed me.

Suddenly I was whirling up and away from the ground. I came to rest on the roof of my building and realized the bird was not a bird at all. It was Batman. He had swung out of the night on a thin rope and grabbed me, carrying me to safety on the roof. My stomach, which felt as if it had been in my throat, settled back in its proper place, but my legs were so wobbly I went down on one knee and looked up at the powerful figure of Batman.

"Wait here," Batman said. Then he was gone, swinging away on his rope into the empty night. But the rope was attached to a building at an angle from us, and that wasn't where Batman wanted to go. He let go of the rope and twisted hard to his left. He fell about ten feet, grabbed a flagpole jutting out from the building across from me.

Bending his knees into his chest, he swung around and around the pole, gaining momentum, then shot straight up and came to land on his feet on the roof of the building where the Joker and his crew were.

Or rather, had been.

The pirate ship was floating up into the night. I could see the faces of the Joker and the pirates peering over the railing near the bow. Batman raced toward the ship. A mooring rope was dangling from it, and Batman leaped and caught hold of it, scrambled up the rope toward the Joker and his crew.

The Joker laughed. Out flashed his chainsaw sword, whacking the rope in half. Batman fell. It was a pretty long drop, and I thought he was going to be mashed flatter than a pie pan, but he coiled himself into a ball and whirled in midair, landed on the roof rolling and came up standing. He turned to glare up at the pirate ship.

The cat that had gotten me into this mess in the first place came out of the dark and rubbed up against Batman's boot. Batman picked up the cat and stroked it, never taking his eyes off the Joker's ship.

The pirate vessel stuck against the moon, like a brooch on a lady's dress. Calling down from the sky, the Joker yelled, "Yo-ho-ho, Bat chump! Arrr, arrr, and all that pirate-type talk."

This was followed by all the pirates yelling, "Arrr, arrr," and more laughter from the Joker and the pirates. The ship gained altitude until it looked as dark and shapeless as a thundercloud.

*   *   *

19

"And just when I thought I was a goner," I said, "Batman grabbed me and swung me onto the roof of our building."

My mother sat down in a kitchen chair and turned white. "Oh, Toby," she said.

"I'm sorry, Mom," I said. "I was trying to do a good deed."

We were in our kitchen, me and Mom, Dad, Commissioner Gordon, Batman, and the cat. The cat was drinking milk out of a saucer on the floor. It didn't seem to have a care in the world.

A few policemen wandered into the kitchen and spoke to Commissioner Gordon, then wandered out. Commissioner Gordon had called them onto the scene after Batman and I showed up and told what had happened and what we knew.

Dad thanked Batman again for saving me and shook his hand for the third time. Commissioner Gordon leaned against the sink counter and looked pale. "Here I am, the Police Commissioner, taking a few hours off, playing a game of cards, while the villain all of Gotham City is hunting for is on the roof across the way, breaking into the museum warehouse to steal priceless treasure. Authentic pirate treasure."

"No way you could have known, Jim," Dad said.

"That's correct," Batman said, "you couldn't have. And even the Police Commissioner deserves a little time off. I only knew to come here because the Joker called me."

"Called you?" Commissioner Gordon asked.

"Signaled me, actually," Batman said. "Much earlier tonight, while on patrol, I saw a light in the sky. I thought it was the Bat Signal at first glance. But it was a Joker Signal. The Joker's face imprinted on a beam of light."

"But why?" Dad asked.

"The Joker doesn't commit crimes for financial gain," Batman said. "That's merely a side benefit. He likes to taunt the police, and especially me. He likes a challenge. I followed the signal to its source. The spotlight was atop the Gotham Novelty Shop, and as was suitable to its location, there was a huge jack-in-the-box on the roof next to the light. It was painted in the Joker's colors, purple, green, red, and white. It was rigged with an electronic eye. It sprang open the moment I swung down on the roof by rope, the jack inside practically leaped at me."

"I'm surprised it didn't blow up in your face," Commissioner Gordon said.

"It was a jack-in-the-box version of the Joker," Batman said. "It had his face and spindly arms and white-gloved hands. In one hand were three large cards, and the cards burst from its hand and fluttered onto the roof. They were numbered one, two, and three. The first was a drawing of pirates digging up treasure. The second was a picture of the classical Greek masks dealing with drama, one showing laughter, the other sadness. The third card was a copy of Goya's painting *The Sleep of Reason Produces Monsters*. And at the top of the third card, drawn in red ink, was a pirate ship with a rope leading away from it, running off the edge of the card."

"What in the world could that mean?" Commissioner Gordon asked.

if there's anything there that might tell us where *The Be-hemoth* is being filmed. If that doesn't work, try another approach. But find out. And once you find out, radio me in the Batmobile. In the meantime, I'll take Toby home. He's been quite a help, but I'm sure his parents are worried about his being out this late."

Mouse turned to me. "I'm quite sorry there wasn't time for refreshments, Mr. Toby."

The man in the mouse mask no longer seemed ridiculous. There was something strong and certain about him.

"It's certainly been a pleasure to meet you," I said. I told Mouse good-bye and shook his paw — uh, hand — and Batman tugged me toward the Batmobile.

CHAPTER FIVE

The Sea Monster

When we reached downtown, Batman let me remove the blindfold. It was his plan to drop me home and pursue any leads Mouse might deliver to him. But as we drove, a strange thing happened to me. I saw a sign for the Gotham Marina, and a flash of lightning went off in my head. That marina sign meant something to me, and it meant something important, but I couldn't remember what it was.

I was still in a relaxed state from the hypnosis, and I decided to use that to my advantage. I concentrated on a red button on the Batmobile's console. I concentrated hard and let my memory drift back. I didn't know where it was drifting to, but I let it go.

It coasted back slowly through the events of the night. Through my adventures on the roof with the Joker and his pirates, and finally it came to rest with me in my room, reading the article on the movie *The Behemoth,* and my favorite actor, Shelly D. Bloon.

I recalled that I had read all of the article, though my

concentration had faded halfway through. But from what I had learned tonight about being hypnotized, I realized that if I had read it, even if my conscious mind only remembered the first half and had been preoccupied with the heat and my wishes to be back home in East Texas, the subconscious part of my mind would retain it all. The article's content would be buried somewhere within my memory. The trick was to make my memory give up what it knew.

I closed my eyes and drifted deeper. I imagined Batman's smooth voice coaxing me back in time, and soon the article was before me. I was back in my room reading it. I could even feel the wind from my fan on my face. Very slowly the words of the article appeared to me, and I knew then why the billboard about the marina had fired off a mental blast of lightning.

The Gotham Marina was where the night shooting was taking place for *The Behemoth!* The article said so. It said an authentic pirate-style city had been built inside the marina, and it discussed how much money had been spent to make it special. But all that mattered now was the location.

I came out of my hypnotic stupor rapidly. "The Gotham Marina, Batman!" I yelled. "That's where the shooting is taking place. I just remembered."

Batman glanced at me. "Toby, there's no time to waste. I've got to go there now. But you've got to stay out of the way. Hear me?"

"Yes, sir," I said. Then, without a word, Batman whipped the steering wheel to the left and the car spun completely about with a screech of tires, and in a fraction of a second, we were facing the other direction.

We darted between a row of honking cars and Batman took a hard right into an alley, and the power of the Batmobile was such that clouds of dust rose up from the alley and plumed against the building walls and rolled behind us in a dark dirty cloud. We shot through the alley and came out on the other side, then wheeled left onto a narrow street.

Batman said, "Hold on, Toby. I'm hitting the boost." Batman hit a switch on the console, and the Batmobile, as if it were a rocket, shot forward with a roar of its engine and a burst of fire.

When I looked to my right, the parked cars at the curb and the apartment buildings were nothing more than a sooty blur.

Instants later, we arrived at the Gotham Marina. The lights around the marina were bright. So bright, neither the moon nor the stars could be seen above. The lights gave the sky a glow the color of a minnow's scales in midday sunlight.

We geared down and blasted up to a metal gate, and a man wearing a guard's uniform came toward us. When he saw what was stopped in front of the gate, his mouth fell open. Of course, he couldn't see inside the Batmobile because of the tinted glass, but he didn't need to see inside to know who was behind the wheel of such a remarkable car.

Batman touched a button and the roof of the car slid back. The air that came in to us smelled faintly of oncoming rain. The nervous guard went through a turnstile next to the gate and came around to the open roof.

"An emergency," Batman said. "I'm coming through."

"Say no more," said the guard. He almost leaped back to the guard house, touched a switch or something inside, and the gate swung open. Batman roared the Batmobile inside the marina as Mouse's voice came over the Batmobile's intercom. "Excuse me, sir. The location of the night shooting for *The Behemoth*. It's included in the computer's memory banks, sir. It's —"

"The Gotham Marina," Batman said into the intercom.

"Well, sir," said Mouse, "if you knew all along, why put me to the bother?"

"Later," Batman replied to Mouse, and the intercom went silent.

"Look," I said, and pointed.

Drifting out of the minnow-silver sky came the Joker's pirate ship. It cut out of the darkness and into the intense light as if it had traveled in time from the olden days of the pirates, as if it had sunk in some long-ago ocean and gone right through the blue-green sea and the dark, slimy bottom and come out in our sky and time. And now, as if still sinking, it was gliding down into the open-roofed amphitheater of the Gotham Marina.

Batman stopped the Batmobile outside the marina, said, "Stay here!" and sprang out of the car and shot out a line tipped with a miniature grappling hook. The line sailed high up and the hook caught on something at the top of the amphitheater I couldn't quite make out, and then, Batman, like a spider on a strand of web, scuttled up the line and came to the top of the amphitheater and went over the lip at about the same time the Joker's pirate ship drifted down and out of sight.

I had watched all of this from the car, and though Batman had told me to stay, I decided that meant stay out of trouble, and that was exactly what I intended to do, but it didn't work that way. Overcome with excitement, I jumped out of the open car and dashed toward the opening of the amphitheater.

There were a lot of people there, camera and makeup people and the like. They were all turned toward the interior of the amphitheater, watching the incredible sight of the Joker's pirate ship. I snuck in without being noticed.

As I squeezed past all the stunned movie people, I was able to see that the Joker's ship had lowered inside the marina but had not touched ground. It was still fairly high up. There were ropes extending from it, and the grappling hooks on the ends of the ropes were fastened to the sides of the amphitheater, which had been made up to look like a city of the pirate era. A huge dinosaur — more of a sea monster, really — stood directly underneath the pirate ship. The sea monster was covered in shiny scales, and long, green strips of seaweed were wound about its body, dangling from it like rags. A bunch of actors, one I recognized as Shelly D. Bloon, stood near the sea monster with their cutlasses drawn. It was obvious they had been interrupted while shooting a scene where the fearless pirates, led by none other than my favorite horror actor, Shelly D. Bloon, were battling the beast. Shelly D. Bloon's sandy blond hair was sticking out from beneath his blue bandanna, and his hard-looking face wore a startled expression. The other actors looked equally surprised.

40

Somewhere to my right I could hear a woman yelling repeatedly, "Cut! Cut! Cut!"

The director of the movie, I figured. But I didn't take time to look. I was too amazed at what was going on in the center of the marina.

The Joker was leaning over the edge of the ship's railing, shaking his cutlass and yelling something I couldn't quite hear. The toy parrot on his shoulder bobbed up and down and swung wildly to the left and right, as if it were about to come unfastened from the Joker's pirate coat.

The sea monster beneath the Joker's ship began to move toward Shelly D. Bloon and the other actors who stood with cutlasses drawn. In the background, the woman was still yelling "Cut! Cut!"

But the action didn't stop. The sea monster came forward with a creak of machinery and bent at the waist. Reaching out with its taloned hands, it grabbed at Shelly D. Bloon.

Shelly D. Bloon danced out of the way and sliced at the mechanical creature with his cutlass. Sparks flew up when his sword hit the metal monster's claws. The other pirate actors scattered. One dropped his cutlass.

On board the ship, the Joker had grabbed a small cannon, and he and Bloody Mary were fastening it to a swivel on the side of the ship. Suddenly the cannon was being twisted down and over the side. I saw a fuse light up and burn quickly. There was an explosion, and out of the mouth of the cannon came a shadowy shape that unfurled into a weighted net attached to a rope. The net went down and around Shelly D. Bloon and pulled taut.

The actor tried to cut his way out with the cutlass, but the net was cinched up too tight. He couldn't move his arms. The rope began to recoil inside the cannon, cranking the net up.

The sea monster came forward and grabbed the net and helped lift it and guide it toward the cannon, but the net tangled on the sea monster's talon, and the beast couldn't shake it free.

"You nincompoop!" the Joker yelled at the sea monster. "Let him go!"

I don't know what happened to me. It was like with the cat. Something had to be done and no one else seemed ready to do it. I forgot my promise to Batman. I darted toward the sea monster. Someone behind me yelled, "Look, that kid!" But no one stopped me. I was running too fast. I got between the sea monster's feet, and reached down and scooped up the cutlass one of the actors had dropped. It wasn't a real cutlass. It was metal, but light as cardboard and dull. It wasn't too heavy for me to turn it sideways and bite the blade, clamp it between my teeth.

A long piece of fake seaweed dangled down from the sea monster's knee, and I grabbed hold of that. It was hard going holding the cutlass between my teeth, even light as it was, but I managed to climb up the seaweed strip and reach the monster's waist. I got hold of another strip of seaweed there and climbed higher. Any time a strip ran out, there was always another to take its place. By the time I got to the sea monster's shoulder, it had worked its talon loose and the net was going the rest of the way up.

Close up like I was, I could see inside one of the monster's eyes. A man was in there working the controls. It was the Joker's pirate henchman, Bony! He had probably pretended to be one of the extras and taken the place of the real operator.

I bolted up the side of the monster's head by hanging on to its shiny scales. I got to the top, and just as the head turned and would have thrown me off, I leaped for the net being cranked up the side of the ship.

I clung to the net with one hand and pulled the cutlass out of my mouth and slashed at the rope holding the net, trying to cut it free. The cutlass was dull and nearly useless, and it hadn't occurred to me what would happen if I did manage to cut it free. It was a long drop. By the time it did occur to me that both Shelly D. Bloon and I would hit the ground like ripe watermelons, it didn't matter. It was too late. The net and Shelly D. Bloon were already at the side of the ship, and Cannon Ball and Bloody Mary were tugging it over the side.

I leaped free of the net and tried to scare the Joker and his two pirates by waving my sword in a threatening manner. Bloody Mary pulled her cutlass from its scabbard so fast I didn't even see it. It seemed to come out of nowhere. She hit my cutlass and sent it winging. I stood there feeling pretty stupid with just my face hanging out.

Cannon Ball rushed me and shoved me toward Bloody Mary. Bloody Mary grabbed me and spun me around and placed her arm across my throat. It was hard to breathe. I struggled, but it was no use.

For the second time in the same night, I had been captured by the Joker.

44

CHAPTER SIX

Home Port

"You again," said the Joker, stalking over and leaning his face into mine. The parrot on his shoulder had fallen so far forward its beak was on the Joker's chest and its tail feathers were sticking straight up.

"My, but you get around," the Joker continued. "Where's your friend, that imbecile Batman?"

I was wondering just that thing, but I said, "You don't scare me."

"Oh," said the Joker. "Well, my little friend, remember, the night is not nearly over. Before it is, you'll be scared. Very, very scared. I promise you that. Tell him, Polly."

The Joker reached for the parrot, discovered it had lost its proper perch. "Oh, Polly," he said and laughed like a crazed Santa Claus. "You do the silliest things. Doesn't she do the silliest things, Cannon Ball?"

Cannon Ball cleared his throat. "Aye, aye, sir, Captain Joker, sir. That Polly, she's quite the cutup, sir. I was just saying to Bloody Mary the other day, that Polly, she breaks me up. She —"

"Shut up!" said the Joker. "That's enough. She's not that funny."

"Of course not, Captain Joker, sir," replied Cannon Ball. "Of course not. Aye, aye, arrr, arrr."

The Joker straightened the parrot carefully, looked at me, winked, and tugged the string attached to Polly's belly.

"Attsss right. The Joker's always right," said the toy parrot, falling forward again and speaking into the Joker's chest.

"That's right, Polly," said the Joker. "I'm always right. Bind the boy, Bloody Mary! Bind him good!"

Bloody Mary put a foot into the back of one of my knees and pushed me to the deck. She pulled my arms behind me and tied my wrists together. This was the second time tonight she'd done such a thing, and frankly, I was seriously tired of it.

As I lay there, being tied up, I turned my head and looked at Shelly D. Bloon, trapped in the net. He tried to give me a brave smile, but it was weak and brief, and considering his face was mashed up against the webbing of the net, not particularly attractive.

When Bloody Mary finished tying me up, the Joker said, "Drop that idiot Bony a line."

Bloody Mary left me where I lay, put her cutlass in its scabbard, and dropped a coiled rope over the side. A long moment later, Bony came scuttling up.

"It took you long enough," the Joker said.

"I couldn't get the trapdoor in the top of the monster's head to open," Bony said. "It was stuck."

"After your performance," said the Joker, "I should have left you there. You almost ripped the net, you fool!"

"Wasn't my fault the sea monster had hooked claws," Bony said.

"Not my fault," the Joker said, mocking Bony. "Not my fault. It's never your fault. No, no. Not your fault. You fool! It's *always* your fault. Ah, never mind. Cast off, you swabbies!"

"Arrr, arrr," said the pirates.

Cannon Ball and Bony rushed to the mooring lines and cut them with their cutlasses. Bloody Mary, cutlass drawn again, stayed near Shelly D. Bloon and me. The Joker scrambled to the great wheel in the front of the ship. He spun the wheel, and the ship turned swiftly and surely.

The Joker touched switches on a panel next to the wheel, and up we rose, out of the brightness of the movie lights, and into the darkness of the night. Higher and higher the ship rose, until the moon and the stars were clearly visible and the smell of distant, oncoming rain became sweeter and cleaner, and the wind was as soft and gentle as the brush of a feather.

It was a beautiful sight, but I didn't feel up to enjoying it. Whatever the Joker had planned for Shelly D. Bloon and me was bound to be unpleasant. And he still had his third crime to commit this night, and it looked as if even Batman would not be able to stop him.

Batman!

Where *was* he?

We drifted on, and the smell of rain grew stronger and the sky became less clear. In the distance, great bolts of yellow-white lightning shot out of the darkness and forked wide and throbbed like neon, hissed like hot branding irons poked into cold water. The air became thick and heavy.

I wondered where we were going and what the Joker had planned for us. I tried to figure what had happened to Batman. He had plenty of time to get over the other side of the amphitheater wall and confront the Joker.

Why hadn't he?

I couldn't come up with answers to any of the questions I asked myself. To keep from being frightened, I tried to concentrate on the last of the Joker's three cards. A copy of the painting by Goya. What had Batman called it? *The Sleep of Reason Produces Monsters?*

What could that mean?

And what about the drawing of a pirate ship with a line, or rope, running off the side of the card, as if it were tied to something out of sight?

Tied!

That's what you did when you brought a ship into a port. You tied it off. Docked it.

Wait! Batman had said Goya was famous for paintings that dealt with war and madness. Nothing suited the Joker more than madness. He was, as my father often said of those who seemed to have poor judgment, a few bricks shy a load.

But what did home port, docking, and madness have to do with one another?

All right, I thought. Home port. That's the pirate connection. That's the place the Joker thinks of as home. The place, that if he were a pirate, he would come back to. As for the madness part . . .

Then it hit me.

The Joker wasn't referring to home. He was referring to where he always ended up, and the reason he always ended up there. A kind of unhappy and unwanted home port for the Joker. The place Batman always sent him back to. A place of madness like Goya painted about.

The great ship turned slightly sideways and I rolled forward against the railing. My face stuck through the rails, and I was looking out at the deep dark fall to the ground. Lights were below us, thicker than the stars. I heard a roll of thunder, and then the lights drifted from our view, and we sailed out over a more deserted area around Gotham.

Finally, our destination came into view. Arkham Asylum, of course. Home port to the criminally insane.

I rolled over and inched my knees under me and was able to sit up with my back to the railing.

"Easy, lad," whispered Shelly D. Bloon. "Don't draw attention to yourself."

I nodded at him, but truthfully, I doubted that it mattered. The Joker was crazy, but he wasn't going to forget us if we merely stayed still.

I watched as new mooring ropes were brought into play and the Joker guided the great pirate ship down toward the roof of the asylum. Bloody Mary and Cannon Ball fastened one end of the ropes to supports on either side of the railings of the ship, then tossed out the grappling hooks. I heard them hit solidly, and I knew we were docked.

I turned to look down at the asylum, and a moment later I was boosted to my feet. The person who pulled me up was none other than the Joker himself. He took hold of my shirt and tugged me so close I couldn't see anything but his teeth, looking like a row of piano keys there in the fading moonlight. Fading, because the clouds were darkening and thickening. The air was full of the smell of rain. Silver-white webs of lightning quivered across the sky. Thunder bowled a strike.

"Leave him alone!" Shelly D. Bloon screamed at the Joker. "He's just a boy, you ridiculous clown. Leave him be."

The Joker, still holding my shirt in both his fists, kicked out and hit Shelly D. Bloon. Mr. Bloon struggled in the net, but it was useless. "You hush, Mr. Horror Star," said the Joker. "I want my little friend to see what I have planned. That," he said, turning me around to face over the railing, "is Arkham Asylum."

"I knew that," I said. "I figured out what your third card meant before we got here." I quickly explained it to him, just to have the pleasure of letting him know he wasn't so smart after all.

"Ah," the Joker said. "You're quite the sharp one, little boy. So smart. But, so you knew where I was going. What of it? Do you know why I've come here? Have you deduced what I have planned?"

I didn't know, so I said nothing.

50

"It's really quite simple," said the Joker. "I'm going to give Batman quite a time. That's what I'm going to do. Arkham Asylum is packed with criminals who hate Batman. Criminals that Batman believes are insane merely because they want to commit nasty, despicable crimes. Can you imagine such a thing? But what if Gotham City was full of Batman's enemies? These so-called criminally insane? The Penguin. The Riddler. Two Face. Clay Face. The Scarecrow. Others. And, of course, the most important, the most dangerous, the smartest, the funniest, the best-looking, and the most modest of all of Batman's enemies: me. Just think of it. Consider how busy Batman will be. Oh, what a mess. Why, poor Mr. Bat won't know if he's coming or going."

The Joker smiled at me. "And I want you to see all these foes of Batman loose, little boy. I want you to see that. It cheers me to know you'll see that, and realize your friend Batman will soon be besieged by all of us who hate him, and wish him the worst. Yes, I want you to see his foes loose. Right before you walk the plank again. Only this time from the deck of my pirate ship high above Gotham City. So high, it'll take you many long seconds to fall. And right behind you will come Shelly D. Bloon."

"Why kidnap him in the first place?" I said. "It doesn't make sense. He hasn't done anything to you. Neither have I."

"Oh, of course it makes sense," said the Joker. He turned to Shelly D. Bloon. "Actually, Mr. Bloon, I needed a pirate connection for my clues to Batman, and having read of your movie filming here, well, the association was obvious. And

51

frankly, sir, I've seen your performances, and might I offer my own simple and highly personal criticism that you stink. Truly, I'm doing you and the world of film quite the favor. I'm putting you and your audiences out of misery. You'll best be remembered as the actor who walked the plank of the Joker's flying pirate ship. Trust me. It'll be a far more famous moment than your role in *The Behemoth* might have been."

"You crazed fiend," said Shelly D. Bloon.

"Oh," said the Joker, "and I've been blaming your scriptwriter for your awful lines. But I discover your ineptness is not restricted to your acting alone. You're quite the awful ad-libber, aren't you. Crazed fiend? How silly. Demented jackal would have been nice. Still stagy, but nicer. Don't you think?"

"I think you're nuts," said Shelly D. Bloon.

The Joker kicked Shelly D. Bloon, but the actor didn't make a sound. He just glared through the webbing of the net.

The Joker put his arm around my shoulders and said, "I wonder, will the two of you scream all the way down? I certainly hope so. What fun is it if you don't scream? Just go off the plank, and SPLAT. That's no fun at all. You will scream, won't you?"

"Never," I said. "I wouldn't give you the pleasure."

The Joker clapped his hands. "Oooohhhh, I love it. I just love it when they talk tough. They always like to talk tough. Until the big time comes. Then they whimper and beg and crawl. Cannon Ball! The battering ram, please!"

Cannon Ball came forward carrying what looked like a

52

bazooka instead of a battering ram. "I wanted you to see this," said the Joker, smiling at the device. "I'm so proud of it. I call it a ram, but actually it fires a teeny-weeny missile. It just makes an awful hole. We'll use it to knock a gap in the asylum roof, little boy. And through that hole, we'll release all those special people I told you about. Oh, I'm giddy just thinking about it."

"Giddy?" said Shelly D. Bloon. "And you talk about my lines. Who writes your dialogue?"

"Oh, Mr. Wit has resurfaced," said the Joker, giving Shelly D. Bloon a hateful look. Then the Joker turned his attention from us and clapped his hands.

A gate in the ship's railing was opened, and out went the landing plank. Cannon Ball and several of the pirates scuttled down it, racing over the roof of Arkham Asylum like ants on a cinnamon roll.

I was so angry, I was about to turn and try to kick the Joker, when out of the corner of my eye, crawling over the roof of the Captain's cabin, I glimpsed an odd shadow. It flowed like oil over the roof, rose up and expanded, a dark blot against a darker sky split by lightning and shaken by thunder.

And by the flash of the lightning, I saw the shadow wasn't a shadow at all.

I almost let out with a cheer.

It was Batman.

CHAPTER SEVEN

At War on the Decks

No sooner had the pirates foamed across the roof of Arkham Asylum than Batman leaped into the midst of those still on the ship. He leaped high and came down on the back of one, driving him so hard into the deck of the ship, it knocked the man unconscious.

Batman bounded to his feet as another pirate attacked, cutlass lifted overhead. As the sword came down, Batman slid in close to the pirate and blocked the man's arm out, grabbed it, then swung in with his back to the pirate, bent, and twisted.

The pirate went flying over Batman's head and slammed hard into the great wheel of the ship. His sword skimmed across the deck and smacked up against the railing next to me. The blow to the wheel didn't knock the pirate unconscious, but he didn't look as if he were in a hurry to jump to his feet.

Bloody Mary tried to skewer Batman on her cutlass. Batman sidestepped as she lunged, grabbed her wrist, and twisted the sword away from her. He slid behind her and kicked her in the rear end, sending her sliding across the deck on her stomach, gathering splinters and finally crashing into the pirate who had recently slammed into the wheel.

"You fools, take him!" the Joker yelled, drawing his cutlass. The sword he pulled this time wasn't the chainsaw weapon. This was an ordinary cutlass, like the other pirates carried. As he brandished it, lightning racked across the sky and flicked light across his sword. The edge of the blade winked with sharpness.

Batman picked up the cutlass he had twisted out of Bloody Mary's hand and smiled. "You think you're such a deadly swordsman," Batman said, "you take me. Come on, Joker. You've got a big mouth. Let's see how you stack up."

The Joker smiled. "Of course, Batman. I'd love that little pleasure. The rest of you," he yelled at his pirates, "stay out of it. This is between me and him . . . unless, of course, I start to lose, and in that case, jump right in. Okay?"

The pirates didn't answer. After seeing Batman handle three of them without any trouble, they were in no hurry to attack him.

The Joker bounced forward on his toes, dodged in and out. He waved his sword wildly. Of course, he wasn't anywhere close to Batman.

"Let's see your moves close up," Batman said.

The Joker, grinning as if it hurt him, edged closer and crossed swords with Batman. They began to duel. Their swords wove in and out. The lightning flashing all about us made the swords sparkle and jump with light. Sparks flew up as the blades met. Batman and the Joker shuffled lightly over the boards, parrying, thrusting, slashing, hacking.

It was obvious Batman was very much in control. He was playing the Joker along, embarrassing him in front of his crew.

I slid along the railing, bent down, reached with my tied hands, and picked up the cutlass that had slid away from the pirate. The way I held it, behind my back, it was difficult to use for cutting myself free.

I leaned it up against the railing, allowing the hilt to touch the floor; then I locked my heels against the hilt and made it secure. I rubbed the leather thong binding my wrists along the blade. In a moment, I was free, and the pirates hadn't noticed. Their attention was on the duel between Batman and the Joker.

I turned and used the sword to cut through the net that held Shelly D. Bloon. In a flash, he was free, brandishing his movie cutlass.

There was a loud rumble of thunder, followed by a hot, forked tongue of lightning that tore across the sky and hit the mainmast, cutting it clean in two. The mast fell forward just as Batman, with a flick of his wrist, disarmed the Joker by knocking the sword from his hand.

At that same instant, the sagging mast swung out and hit Batman in the back, knocking him down and into the Joker. Striking his chin against the Joker's knee, Batman went down with a grunt and lay sprawled on the deck, dazed.

Below me, I heard the "battering ram," as the Joker called it, going off. In only minutes, Batman's most fright-

ening enemies would be free. And there was no one to stop them.

The Joker recovered his cutlass. He smiled. He raised the blade to finish off Batman. I yelled and jumped forward, slashing the air with my sword. "Hey, me hearties!" I cried. "I'll run ye through."

I had heard that in a pirate movie. I wasn't exactly sure what it meant, but I thought it sounded good.

The Joker froze his blow in midair. He turned and looked at me. He and the pirates stared at me as if I were an amazing joke that had flopped.

Shelly D. Bloon went prancing past me light as a ballet dancer. "*En garde!*" he yelled at the Joker, and in a flash they were knocking swords together. Shelly D. Bloon drove the Joker away from Batman, toward the railing of the ship. Shelly D. Bloon looked great. He wasn't just a movie star — by golly, he was a real hero.

The remaining pirates rushed forward to aid the Joker, but Batman, having had a moment to recover, leaped to his feet and spun to face them.

The pirates went stiff as statues.

Batman's back was to me, but I figured his face — what could be seen of it beneath his mask — must have appeared pretty grim, considering the way all those armed pirates were standing around with their mouths open.

Batman still held the cutlass, but he amazed me by tossing it aside. He relaxed and stretched to greater height.

"Now I'm irritated," he said.

"Watch out, Batman!" I yelled.

Bloody Mary had recovered and gotten hold of a harpoon

and was sneaking up on Batman, ready to spear him. She tossed the harpoon.

Batman ducked as casually as if he were bending to tie his shoe. The harpoon went over his back and into the middle of the pirates, who scattered like chickens in a hailstorm. The harpoon slammed into the deck, stuck, vibrated.

Batman jumped forward, grabbed Bony by the throat and the knee of the pants, swung him around and into the others, using him like a club. Pirates flew left and right.

It only took a moment of that for the pirates to toss down their swords, screaming for mercy. Batman dropped the dazed Bony and spoke to the pirates as if he were talking to trained dogs, "Stay where you are."

"Okay, Batman," said Bloody Mary, rubbing her head where Bony had slammed into her. "We give up."

"Get their swords, Toby," Batman said.

I raced forward and collected the swords and the harpoon. When I had them all, I carried them over to the railing and dropped them in a heap.

The Joker and Shelly D. Bloon were still dueling. The actor was having fun. He was leaping and capering about, spinning behind the Joker and slapping him on the backside with the flat of his fake sword. He was, in fact, playing pirate.

Batman walked right into their midst and said, "Pardon me. Fun's over." Batman caught the Joker's wrist, turned into him, and landed a solid punch to the Joker's jaw. The Joker's feet flew out from under him and he went out like a match in a high wind. He lay sprawled on the deck with his tongue hanging out of the corner of his mouth.

"You two watch them," Batman said as we heard yet another boom of the "battering ram" from below. "I've got to stop an escape."

Batman glanced over the railing to see what was happening. Then he raced to the wheel of the ship and yelled to me. "I need your help, Toby! Kick the landing plank aside!"

I darted for the plank and did just that. It fell to the roof of the asylum with a clatter. I leaned over the side of the ship for a look.

Cannon Ball and his helpers were clustered on the roof. Cannon Ball was holding the "battering ram." He had knocked a large hole in the roof, but apparently the roof had been thicker than the Joker had anticipated, and another shot had been required. One of the pirates was tossing a rope ladder over the lip of the hole they had made and was about to descend and free the mad criminals who lived there.

But the great pirate ship began to move. It moved forward and down.

Cannon Ball looked up. A flash of lightning showed his features to me clearly. He was terrified. The pirate ship was coming down on top of him.

"Run!" he yelled. But there was nowhere to go. Neither direction the pirates retreated to would be good enough. The ship was too large and was coming down too fast. In a moment it would be on top of them.

"Inside!" yelled Cannon Ball, and the pirates raced to descend the rope ladder that led into the asylum. And Batman, very gently, very smoothly, set the great airship down on the top of the hole.

"Toby," Batman called to me.

I ran to his side. "Aye, aye, Captain Batman, sir."

Batman grinned. "Hold the wheel while I secure the ship with mooring lines."

"Aye, aye, Captain, sir," I said.

"And Toby," he said, "thanks for saving my life. Thanks to you and Shelly D. Bloon."

"Aye, aye, Captain, sir. And thanks for saving our lives."

I took hold of the wheel, and Batman went about his business. I turned and looked at the pirates, fearing they might take this chance to escape. But no. They were bunched together like grapes on a vine. The fight was out of them. Shelly D. Bloon was standing in front of them, bouncing on his toes, slashing his sword in the air, making threatening gestures.

"This'll teach you sea dogs to mess with Batman and Shelly D. Bloon," the actor said.

"And Toby," I said.

Shelly D. Bloon glanced at me out of the corner of his eye and smiled. "Yeah, and Toby."

The lightning cracked again, and this time the rain, which had been threatening us all night, came down, hard and cool.

I didn't mind at all.

CHAPTER EIGHT
All's Well

We were heroes. Next afternoon, Shelly D. Bloon and I were given medals by Commissioner Gordon at City Hall. He gave them to us at a downtown ceremony. The Mayor and his staff attended. And so did my parents and Batman and a large number of the police department.

We were on TV, and the next day our pictures were on the front page of the *Gotham Times*.

If anyone deserved a medal, it was Batman, of course, but as he explained it to me, "It's just part of my job."

When the ceremony was over, Batman walked with me and my parents and Shelly D. Bloon out to our car. As we were about to get inside, I said, "What happened at the marina, Batman? I saw you go over the top, but after that, I didn't see you again. Not until the ship docked at Arkham Asylum."

"As I was going over the wall of the marina," Batman said, "it occurred to me, as it did to you, what the third clue meant. I wanted to make sure that the Joker didn't have plans for more henchmen to meet him at Arkham Asylum, and I feared he might have inside help. Someone who wasn't an inmate, but was on his payroll."

"In other words," Shelly D. Bloon said, "you wanted to make a clean sweep?"

"Correct," Batman said. "Turned out the Joker didn't have any more henchmen, no one helping him on the inside, but I wanted to be sure. I didn't want any cronies of the Joker free. And I didn't want anyone there who might help the other criminals escape at a later date. So when I saw neither of you were in immediate danger, but were only being captured, I decided to jump aboard the pirate ship and wait. The way the back of the pirate ship touched the marina, I was able to board it without anyone seeing me. Then, in flight, I worked my way down the side of the ropes, and . . . you know the rest."

Batman shook my hand and the hands of Shelly D. Bloon and my parents, then waved good-bye and walked off to the Batmobile.

Dad gave Shelly D. Bloon a lift to his apartment in an expensive part of Gotham City, then we drove home.

I guess you could say that was it.

Oh, a little later on, Shelly D. Bloon fixed it so I could go on the set of *The Behemoth* any time I wanted. I even got to ride inside the head of the mechanical sea monster, and the operator let me try out the controls. That was great!

When the filming was over, Shelly D. Bloon gave my parents and me free passes to the premiere of the movie. We had the best seats in the house and got to sit with a lot

of movie stars and the director of the picture. She was very nice.

Shelly D. Bloon calls me now and then, though not quite as often as at first. That's understandable. He travels all over the world making motion pictures. *The Behemoth* was a big success. I wonder if the Joker will eventually watch it on videocassette in Arkham Asylum.

We named the stray cat, which we kept, Behemoth, after the movie. He's not much of a behemoth, but we liked the name.

Now that it's all over, my life has pretty much gone back to normal. The days are still hot and I haven't made any friends other than Shelly D. Bloon and Batman here in Gotham City, but in time I probably will.

Until then, however, I can think about the time I met my favorite actor, Shelly D. Bloon, and saved Batman's life, and helped him solve one of his more important cases.

Joe R. Lansdale is the author of many novels for adults, including *Cold in July, Savage Season,* and *The Drive-In.* He has also written many short stories and a novel, *Captured by the Engines,* which feature Batman, and has recently written the script for an episode of the upcoming animated television series about the Caped Crusader.

Mr. Lansdale lives in Nacogdoches, Texas, with his wife and two children.